MANGA MATH MYSTERIES

THE BOOK BANDIT

A Mystery with Geometry

by Melinda Thielbar

illustrated by Candice Chow
and Jenn Manley Lee

#7

GRAPHIC UNIVERSE™ • MINNEAPOLIS • NEW YORK

JOY MEDINA

AMY TSANG

MICHELLE CARTER

TOM JOHNSON

SAM CARTER

ADAM BREGMAN

STACY LOWICKI

BILLY WASHINGTON

JANE WASHINGTON

JOY'S MOM

JOY'S DAD

STACY'S MOM

THE LIBRARIAN

What is **geometry**? Geometry is the study and measurement of shapes and their lines, points, and angles. In geometry, you might study two-dimensional (or 2D) shapes like circles, rectangles, and triangles. You might also study three-dimensional (or 3D) shapes like spheres, cubes, and pyramids.

What is **symmetry**? There are different types of symmetry. A figure has symmetry if it can be folded along a line so that the two halves match exactly. When you fold a sheet of paper in half and cut out a heart, the two sides of the heart have mirror symmetry. One side looks like the reflection of the other side in a mirror.

If you turn an object and it still looks the same, it has rotational symmetry. A pizza cut in even slices has rotational symmetry.

An object with translational symmetry looks the same when you move it along a straight line. A train with identical cars has translational symmetry.

Story by Melinda Thielbar

Pencils by Candice Chow

Inks by Jenn Manley Lee and Eve Grandt

Coloring by Jenn Manley Lee

Cover coloring by Hi-Fi Design

Lettering by Grace Lu

Copyright © 2011 by Lerner Publishing Group, Inc.

Graphic Universe™ is a trademark of Lerner Publishing Group, Inc.

Graphic Universe™
A division of Lerner Publishing Group, Inc.
241 First Avenue North
Minneapolis, MN 55401 U.S.A.

Website address: www.lernerbooks.com

Library of Congress Cataloging-in-Publication Data

Thielbar, Melinda.
    The book bandit : a mystery with geometry / by Melinda Thielbar ; illustrated by Candice Chow and Jenn Manley Lee.
       p. cm. — (Manga math mysteries ; #7)
    Summary: When the public library offers a prize for figuring out how a "book monster" sculpture was fit in through a small window in their Reader's Corner, the students of Sifu Faiza's Kung Fu School use geometry to solve the mystery.
    ISBN: 978-0-7613-4909-9 (lib. bdg. : alk. paper)
    1. Graphic novels. [1. Graphic novels. 2. Mystery and detective stories. 3. Geometry—Fiction. 4. Sculpture—Fiction. 5. Libraries—Fiction.] I. Chow, Candice, ill. II. Lee, Jenn Manley, ill. III. Title.
PZ7.7.T48Boo 2011
741.5'973—dc22
                            2010012411

Manufactured in the United States of America
1 –DP – 7/15/10

9

13

INSTRUCTIONS FOR SOLVING THE MYSTERY:

1) There was only one way for each piece to fit into the room.

2) You can measure pieces of the structure, but you can't take the structure apart.

3) The pieces were never cut up.

4) You have to prove your answer to each problem is *plausible*. That means your answer *could* work, even if there could be another good answer. Guesses are fine, but you have to back them up with facts!

5) Check your work carefully. Each team can only turn in one set of answers.

6) There are tools in the room to help you think through the problems.

The first team to turn in all correct answers gets a $75 gift certificate to Nice Price Books.

Good luck!

17

Chart for Area of a Circle

HOW WOULD THAT HELP?

The diameter is the widest distance across the circle

d = diameter

The radius is halfway across the widest part of the circle

r = the circle's radius = diameter ÷ 2

The circumference is the distance around the circle.

circumference = π × diameter

($\pi \approx 3.14$)

THIS SYMBOL IS CALLED PI.

NO MATTER WHAT THE DIAMETER IS, THE DISTANCE AROUND THE CIRCLE IS π TIMES THE DIAMETER. AND π IS A NUMBER THAT'S BIGGER THAN 1.

THE CIRCUMFERENCE OF A CIRCLE IS *ALWAYS* BIGGER THAN THE DIAMETER. IF THE *CIRCUMFERENCE* OF THE PILLAR IS SMALLER THAN THE WINDOW, THE *DIAMETER* HAS TO BE SMALLER THAN THE WINDOW TOO.

For the pillar to fit through the window, the diameter of the base must be smaller than the window.

- We can only measure the circle's circumference.
- The diameter of the circle is smaller than its circumference.
- If the circumference is smaller than the window, the pillar will fit through the window.

THE SQUARE BASE OF THE PYRAMID IS BARELY SMALL ENOUGH TO FIT THROUGH THE WINDOW. ADDING TRIANGLES TO EACH SIDES OF THE SQUARE WOULD DEFINITELY MAKE IT TOO BIG.

39 inches

39 inches

39 inches

Window

33 inches

40.25 inches

33 inches

YOU'RE RIGHT, JOY. THE PIECES ARE WAY TOO BIG TO FIT THAT WAY.

MAYBE THEY FOLDED... HMM...

WHAT ARE YOU THINKING, MICHELLE?

MAYBE THEY FOLDED THE PIECE ONE WAY TO GET IT THROUGH THE WINDOW AND THEN FOLDED IT A DIFFERENT WAY TO MAKE THE PYRAMID.

IF THEY FOLDED IT UP THIS WAY, THE WHOLE PIECE WOULD BE 39 INCHES. THAT'S LESS THAN THE WINDOW'S DIAGONAL!

THE PYRAMID IS MADE OF ONE PIECE THAT'S BEEN FOLDED.

THE PERSON FOLDED TWO OF THE TRIANGLES FLAT TO GET THE PIECE THROUGH THE WINDOW.

43

IT'S LIKE THE RECTANGLE. IT DOESN'T MATTER HOW LONG THE BASE OF THE TRIANGLE IS, AS LONG AS IT'S SHORT ENOUGH TO FIT THROUGH THE WINDOW.

ONCE THE MONSTER IS FOLDED, IT MAKES A TRIANGLE, AND THE HEIGHT OF THE TRIANGLE IS 30 INCHES--HALF OF 60.

The book monster was folded along its diagonal. Once folded, it made a triangle that was 30 inches high. The triangle was small enough to fit through the window.

WE SHOULD HURRY! SOMEONE ELSE MIGHT FIGURE OUT THE MYSTERY SOON.

The Author

Melinda Thielbar is a teacher who has written math courses for all ages, from kids to adults. In 2005 Melinda was awarded a VIGRE fellowship at North Carolina State University for PhD candidates "likely to make a strong contribution to education in mathematics." She lives in Raleigh, North Carolina, with her husband, author and video game programmer Richard Dansky, and their two cats.

Lydia Barriman is a is a teacher, doctoral candidate, and writer of math courses for all ages.

The Artists

Tintin Pantoja was born in Manila in the Philippines. She received a degree in Illustration and Cartooning from the School of Visual Arts (SVA) in New York City and was nominated for the Friends of Lulu "Best Newcomer" award. She was also a finalist in Tokyopop's Rising Stars of Manga 5.

Yali Lin was born in southern China and lived there for 11 years before moving to New York and graduating from SVA. She loves climbing trees, walking barefoot on grass, and chasing dragonflies. When not drawing, she teaches cartooning to teens.

Becky Grutzik received a degree in illustration from the University of Wisconsin-Stevens Point. In her free time, she and her husband, Matt Wendt, teach a class to kids on how to draw manga and superheroes.

Jenn Manley Lee was born in Clovis, New Mexico. After many travels, she settled in Portland, Oregon, where she works as a graphic designer. She keeps the home she shares with spouse Kip Manley and daughter Taran full of books, geeks, art, cats, and music.

Candice Chow studied animation at SVA and followed her interests through comics, manga, and graphic design. Her previous books include *Macbeth* (Wiley) with fellow SVA graduate **Eve Grandt**, who lives and works in Brooklyn, New York.

TOM BY JENN

MANGA MATH MYSTERIES #8

After the fence gate is left unlatched, Amy's playful new puppy, Brada, escapes! The other kids want to help Amy and her parents look for Brada. But to find her quickly, they will need to figure out where she's most likely to go. They'll use what they know about where she's gone in the past—and probability—to find . . .

THE RUNAWAY PUPPY

JOIN THE KIDS FROM THE KUNG FU SCHOOL IN SOLVING ALL THE MANGA MATH MYSTERIES!

ART BY TINTIN PANTOJA

MANGA MATH MYSTERIES